For Kaia, my Wolf Baby.
—A.D.

For the Kitten, the O Bear,
the Twookie,
and also for Marlow's
mum and dad—L.D.D.
—Z.O.

Text copyright © 2015 by Ame Dyckman • Illustrations copyright © 2015 by Zachariah OHora • Cover art © 2015 by Zachariah OHora • Cover design by Saho Fujii • Cover copyright © 2015 Hachette Book Group, Inc. • All rights reserved. In accordance with the U.S. Copyright Act of 1976, the scanning, uploading, and electronic sharing of any part of this book without the permission of the publisher is unlawful piracy and theft of the author's intellectual property. If you would like to use material from the book (other than for review purposes), prior written permission must be obtained by contacting the publisher at permissions@hbgusa.com. Thank you for your support of the author's rights. • Little, Brown and Company • Hachette Book Group • 1290 Avenue of the Americas, New York, NY 10104 • Visit our website at lb-kids.com • Little, Brown and Company is a division of Hachette Book Group, Inc. The Little, Brown name and logo are trademarks of Hachette Book Group, Inc. • The publisher is not responsible for websites (or their content) that are not owned by the publisher. • First Edition: February 2015 • Library of Congress Cataloging-in-Publication Data • Dyckman, Ame. • Wolfie the bunny / Ame Dyckman ; illustrated by Zachariah OHora. • pages cm • Summary: When her parents find a baby wolf on their doorstep and decide to raise him as their own, Dot is certain he will eat them all up until a surprising encounter with a bear brings them closer together. • ISBN 978-0-316-22614-1 (hardcover) • [1. Wolves—Fiction. 2. Rabbits—Fiction. 3. Animals, Infancy—Fiction. 4. Adoption—Fiction.] I. OHora, Zachariah, illustrator. II. Title. • PZ7.D9715Wol 2015 • [E]—dc23 • 2013034213 • 10 • APS • Printed in China

WOLFIE
THE BUNNY

L B

Little, Brown and Company
New York   Boston

Written by **Ame Dyckman**   Illustrated by **Zachariah OHora**

The Bunny family came home to find
a bundle outside their door.

They peeked. They gasped. It was a baby wolf!
"He's adorable!" said Mama. "He's ours!" said Papa.

"HE'S GOING TO EAT US ALL UP!"

said Dot.

But Mama and Papa were too smitten to listen.

Wolfie slept through the night.

Dot did not.

Mama served carrots for breakfast.
"He likes them!" said Mama.

"He's a good eater!" said Papa.

"Speaking of eating," said Dot,

"HE'S GOING TO EAT US ALL UP!"

But Mama and Papa were too busy taking pictures to listen.

Dot's friends came by to see the baby.

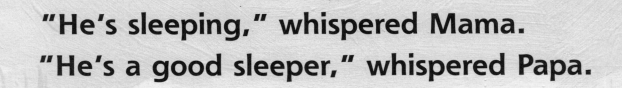

"He's sleeping," whispered Mama.
"He's a good sleeper," whispered Papa.

"HE'S GOING TO EAT US ALL UP!" they screamed.

"No kidding," said Dot. "Let's play at your house."

For the first time, Wolfie cried.

But Dot was too far away to hear him.

When Dot returned,
Wolfie was waiting.

Everywhere Dot went,
Wolfie went, too.

"He's drooling on me!"
said Dot.

"He's a good drooler!"
said Papa.

The days passed, and Wolfie grew.
So did his appetite.

When Mama opened the cupboard, she got a surprise.
"The carrots!" said Mama. "They're gone!"
"Oh no!" said Papa.

"HE ATE THEM ALL UP!"

said Dot.

Dot fetched the carrot bag.
But she did not get far.

Wolfie and Dot went to the Carrot Patch.

Dot was picking one last carrot when Wolfie's mouth opened wide.

"I *knew* it!" cried Dot.

"On guard!"

But Wolfie wasn't looking at Dot.

"DINNER!"

roared the bear.

It was Dot's chance to run away.

Instead, she ran forward.

"Let him go!" Dot demanded.

"Or... I'LL EAT YOU ALL UP!"

The bear blinked. "You're a bunny," he said.

"I'M A HUNGRY BUNNY,"

said Dot.

"But I'm bigger than you,"
   said the bear.

"I'LL START ON YOUR TOES,"
said Dot.

Dot relaxed as the bear ran away.
"We're safe!" she said.

Then Wolfie pounced.

"Come on, little brother.
Let's go home and eat."

ARTIST'S NOTE

The illustrations in this book were painted in acrylic on 90-pound acid-free Stonehenge paper. The setting is an homage to our former neighborhood of Park Slope, Brooklyn, where we had a little "garden level" apartment—which is really New York real estate–speak for "You live in a basement." But what better place for a bunny family to live?

It was a sweet time for us as new parents, and I'm glad to capture some of that feeling in the art for this wonderful story.

—*Zachariah OHora*

AUTHOR'S NOTE

My daughter was an adorable toddler—except when she was tired. Then she transformed. "She's a Wolf Baby!" her father and I would say. (Quietly, so she wouldn't hear us.) And that gave me an idea...

—*Ame Dyckman*

This book was edited by Alvina Ling and Bethany Strout and designed by Saho Fujii. The production was supervised by Erika Schwartz, and the production editor was Barbara Bakowski. This book was printed on Gold Sun woodfree. The text was set in Shannon and the display type was hand-lettered.